Remembering ETHAN

For Judy, with love—*LN*
For John, because you have the biggest heart—*TNB*

Books for Kids From the
American Psychological Association

Magination Press is a registered trademark of the American
Psychological Association. Order books at maginationpress.
org, or call 1-800-374-2721.

Book design by Gwen Grafft

Printed by Worzalla, Stevens Point, WI

Library of Congress Cataloging-in-Publication Data

Names: Newman, Lesléa, author. | Bishop, Tracy, illustrator.
Title: Remembering Ethan / by Lesléa Newman ; illustrated
  by Tracy Nishimura Bishop.
Description: [Washington, DC] : Magination Press, [2020] |
  Audience: Ages 4-8. | Summary: A young girl misses her
  deceased brother and wants to talk about him, and she does
  not understand why her parents do not even want to
  mention his name.
Identifiers: LCCN 2019025134 | ISBN 9781433831133
  (hardcover)
Subjects: CYAC: Death—Fiction. | Grief—Fiction. |
  Brothers—Fiction.
Classification: LCC PZ7.N47988 Rg 2020 | DDC [E]—dc23
LC record available at https://s/2019025134

Manufactured in the United States of America
10 9 8 7 6 5 4 3 2 1

Remembering

ETHAN

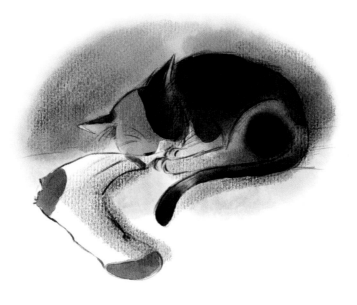

By Lesléa Newman

Illustrated by
Tracy Nishimura Bishop

Magination Press • Washington, DC • American Psychological Association

My big brother Ethan was so tall, he had to duck
his head when he walked through the front door.
My big brother Ethan was so handsome, somebody once
thought he was a movie star and asked for his autograph.

My big brother Ethan was so strong, he could
carry me under one arm and Buttons under the other
arm just like we were two big bags of groceries.

But that was before Ethan went away.

That was before Ethan died.

Mommy won't talk about Ethan. As soon as I say his name, she says, "Sarah, don't," and turns her head away.

Daddy won't talk about Ethan either. As soon as I say his name, he says, "Sarah, please," and folds his arms and sighs.

Buttons is the only one who misses Ethan as much as I do. Buttons carries one of Ethan's socks around in her mouth and kneads it with her paws. Buttons sleeps curled up in a circle on Ethan's bed with her whiskers resting on her tail. Sometimes I sleep there, too.

This morning Mommy was standing at the stove cooking breakfast.
"Do you want your eggs scrambled or fried?" she asked.
I said, "I want them funny-side up," like Ethan used to say.
Mommy smacked her egg against the side of
the frying pan so hard, the shell shattered into
a hundred pieces and egg dripped all over the floor.

I ran upstairs to Ethan's room. Buttons was sleeping on his bed all curled up in a circle with her whiskers resting on her tail. "I miss Ethan," I told Buttons. I hadn't said his name out loud in a long time. "Ethan, ETHAN, ETHAN

I sat down at Ethan's desk and took out some markers and paper. I wrote Ethan's name in all capital letters. I wrote Ethan's name in all small letters. I wrote Ethan's name in yellow, blue, orange, red, and green.

When I was finished writing, I took out a new
piece of paper and drew a picture of Ethan
giving Buttons and me a double piggy-back ride.

I carried my picture into the kitchen and
hung it up on the refrigerator.

When Mommy saw what I had drawn, she burst
into tears and ran upstairs. Daddy stood up so fast
his chair crashed to the floor and he ran upstairs, too.

I stomped back up to Ethan's room. "Doesn't anyone but Buttons and me miss Ethan?" I yelled as loudly as I could. "Doesn't anyone but Buttons and me even *remember* Ethan?" I yelled even louder. Then I slammed the door, lay down on Ethan's bed next to Buttons, and pulled the covers over my head.

A little while later, I came downstairs and found Mommy and Daddy sitting on the living room couch. My picture of Ethan was hanging on the wall, right over the fireplace.

"Are you still mad at me?" I asked.

"We were never mad at you," said Daddy. "We were just too hurt to talk about Ethan yet. I love your picture."
"It's beautiful," Mommy said. "I'm glad you drew it. It will help us remember Ethan."

Hearing Daddy and Mommy say my big brother's name out loud made me feel happy and sad at the same time.

"Come here, Sarah," Mommy said.
I sat down between her and Daddy.
There was a big book on the coffee table.

"What's that?" I asked.
"Why don't you open it and see?" answered Daddy.

I opened the book.
"Look, Sarah," Mommy pointed.
"There's Ethan holding you the very
first day he became a big brother."

"Look, Sarah," Daddy pointed. "There's Ethan lighting
candles on a birthday cake he baked just for you."

"He'd always say, 'Want to cut a rug?'" Mommy
remembered, "and then he'd take my hand and twirl me
around the room until I was out of breath from laughing."

"He'd always say, 'I challenge you to a duel,'"
Daddy remembered, "and then we'd roll up our
sleeves and go at it until I gave in and cried 'uncle.'"

"He'd always say, 'Anyone want to horse around?'" I remembered, "and then I'd put my arms around his neck and say, 'Giddy-up,' and he'd whinny and we'd ride away."

We sat there a while longer, remembering Ethan.
I curled against Mommy and rested my head on
her shoulder. Daddy held my hand. Buttons came
downstairs with Ethan's sock in her mouth and
jumped into my lap. She was remembering, too.

Mommy wiped her eyes. Daddy blew his nose.
Buttons purred. My stomach growled.
"Who wants breakfast?" Mommy asked.
"I do," I said.
"I do," said Daddy.

While Mommy cooked, I helped Daddy set the table.
Then the three of us sat down and ate our eggs
funny-side up, just the way my big brother, Ethan, liked them.

Note to Readers

By Elizabeth McCallum, PhD

Remembering Ethan is a touching and sometimes heartbreaking story of one family's journey to cope with the loss of a child. The story is told from the perspective of the young Sarah, who is struggling to come to terms with her older brother Ethan's death, while simultaneously adjusting to the sadness that seems to have overtaken her parents. Although no family hopes to find themselves in a situation of needing this book, it can be a valuable resource for helping you talk to your children about love, death, and the stages of grief. By helping children relate their feelings to those experienced by Sarah in the aftermath of Ethan's death, you can encourage them to talk about questions and fears they may have, as well as learn tools and strategies for coping with those feelings.

Childhood Grief

Grieving is an important process that allows us to accept that a loved one has died, deal with our feelings surrounding the person's death, and, ultimately, say goodbye. Like adults, children express their grief in a myriad of different ways. Some children may exhibit brief, intense outbursts of emotion. Others may experience behavioral changes, like increased distractibility, sleep disturbances, or periods of anxiety or depression. Still others may experience physical symptoms like stomachaches or headaches. Some children may experience a combination of many of these symptoms while some may not show any discernible signs of sadness or grief. The degree to which a child displays signs of grief often depends on the closeness of their relationship to the person who has died, the age of the child, and the behavior of those around them.

When a family loses a child, the family is changed immediately and forever. The surviving child's grief is likely to be intertwined with the grief of the parents and other members of the family. Children of different ages tend to display signs of grief in different ways. Because young children have a less well-developed understanding of death, they may seem to be impacted less than older children. School-aged children may experience feelings of guilt upon surviving their siblings, as well as intense worries that they or their surviving loved ones may die.

How You Can Help

Regardless of their age, whenever children lose a sibling, they will need help processing their grief and adjusting to life without their sibling.

Speak honestly about the situation. Talk to your child about what has happened straightforwardly and honestly, using developmentally-appropriate language. Phrases like "her body stopped working" are easier for young children to comprehend than "we lost your sister this morning." Children may interpret the latter to mean that she is temporarily lost and may one day be found. Encourage your child to ask questions; answer their questions as simply and honestly as possible.

Talk to your child's teachers and coaches. Let your child's teachers, coaches, and religious leaders know what has happened. These people will be important supports to your child as they move through the grieving process at school and in other relevant spaces beyond the home environment.

Encourage your child to express their feelings. Let your child see and hear you express your feelings, and tell them that expressing our feelings is a way that we cope with what has happened. Make sure they know that everyone expresses their grief differently, and try to find ways that they feel comfortable doing so. Drawing pictures, journaling, and talking to a close friend or counselor are all healthy ways of expressing emotions. Some children may find joining support groups for siblings who have experienced similar losses to be particularly helpful.

Encourage memories. Part of grieving is the long and difficult process of coming to terms with the fact that the loved one is gone forever. This can be particularly difficult for children. Memories can be powerful in helping your child through this part of the grieving process. Help your child find ways to remember their sibling, like looking at photos, telling stories, or creating a memory box filled with items that remind your child of them. These can all be powerful ways of helping your child to process their grief and feel connected to their sibling.

Take care of yourself. One of the most important ways you can help your child after the death of a sibling is by taking care of yourself. Oftentimes, parents who have lost one child are so focused on keeping the family running that they forget to take time for their own grieving. Things you can do to take care of yourself include eating properly, getting adequate sleep, accepting help from friends and family to get through your day-to-day routine tasks, and finding someone you trust to talk to about what has happened.

Seek professional help when needed. If you find that you or your child's feelings of sadness or changes in behavior are not improving over time or are worsening, do not hesitate to seek help from a mental health professional. Your family has undergone one of life's most unimaginable losses, and professional support is available for you.

Elizabeth McCallum, PhD, is an associate professor in the school psychology program at Duquesne University, as well as a Pennsylvania certified school psychologist. She is the author of many scholarly journal articles and book chapters on topics including academic and behavioral interventions for children and adolescents.

About the Author

Lesléa Newman has created more than 70 books for readers of all ages including the picture books, *Gittel's Journey: An Ellis Island Story*, *Sparkle Boy*, and *Ketzel, The Cat Who Composed*. Her literary awards include the Massachusetts Book Award, the Association of Jewish Libraries Sydney Taylor Award, and the American Library Association Stonewall Honor. She lives in Massachusetts. Visit lesleakids.com and follow her on Twitter @lesleanewman.

About the Illustrator

Tracy Nishimura Bishop is an illustrator of more than 20 picture and chapter books. She grew up on a U.S. Army base in Japan and has always loved drawing. Tracy has a degree in graphic design with a focus on illustration and animation from San Jose State University. She currently lives in San Jose, California. Visit tracybishop.com and follow her on Instagram and Twitter @tracybishopart.

About Magination Press

Magination Press is the children's book imprint of the American Psychological Association. Through APA's publications, the association shares with the world mental health expertise and psychological knowledge. Magination Press books reach young readers and their parents and caregivers to make navigating life's challenges a little easier. It's the combined power of psychology and literature that makes a Magination Press book special. Visit www.maginationpress.org.